MARGATE CITY PUBLIC LIBRARY

8100 ATLANTIC AVENUE

MARGATE CITY, NJ 08402

(609) 822-4700

www.margatelibrary.org

1. Most items may be checked out for two weeks and renewed for the same period. Additional restrictions may apply to high-demand items.

2. A fine is charged for each day material is not returned according to the above rule. No material will be issued to any person incurring such a fine until it has been paid.

3. All damage to material beyond reasonable wear and all losses shall be paid for.

4. Each borrower is responsible for all items checked out on his/her library card and for all fines accruing on the same.

OCT   2021

-My Family-
My First-Generation Family

by Claudia Harrington
illustrated by Zoe Persico

Looking Glass Library

An Imprint of Magic Wagon
abdopublishing.com

To my loving parents that grace me with never ending love, support, laughs, and a cozy bed when I visit. —ZP

abdopublishing.com

Published by Magic Wagon, a division of ABDO, PO Box 398166, Minneapolis, Minnesota 55439. Copyright © 2018 by Abdo Consulting Group, Inc. International copyrights reserved in all countries. No part of this book may be reproduced in any form without written permission from the publisher. Looking Glass Library™ is a trademark and logo of Magic Wagon.

Printed in the United States of America, North Mankato, Minnesota.
052017
092017

THIS BOOK CONTAINS RECYCLED MATERIALS

Written by Claudia Harrington
Illustrated by Zoe Persico
Edited by Heidi M.D. Elston
Art Directed by Candice Keimig

Publisher's Cataloging-in-Publication Data

Names: Harrington, Claudia, author. | Persico, Zoe, illustrator.
Title: My first-generation family / by Claudia Harrington ; illustrated by Zoe Persico.
Description: Minneapolis, MN : Magic Wagon, 2018. | Series: My family
Summary: Lenny follows Manny for a school project and learns about a classmate from an immigrant family.
Identifiers: LCCN 2017930509 | ISBN 9781532130182 (lib. bdg.) | ISBN 9781614798330 (ebook) | ISBN 9781614798408 (Read-to-me ebook)
Subjects: LCSH: Family--Juvenile fiction. | Family life--Juvenile fiction. | Immigrants--Juvenile fiction.
Classification: DDC [E]--dc23
LC record available at http://lccn.loc.gov/2017930509

When the last bell rang, Lenny shot out of his seat. "Just a minute, Lenny," said Miss Fish. "You're going home with Manny, remember? He's Student of the Week."

Miss Fish handed Lenny the class camera as Manny joined him.

"Ready?" Manny asked as he kneed a soccer ball.
Click!

"Sure," said Lenny. "How do you get home?"

"Take a look," said Manny when they got in front of school.

"Whoa!" said Lenny. "Fan-cy!"

Click!

Manny chuckled. "Nah. It's just my dad. Hi, Papa!"
"Cool!" said Lenny.

"Hop in," said Papa. "We have to stop for dinner on the way home."
Click!

Lenny's eyes swelled to the size of small soccer balls.

"Does your dad buy you takeout?"

"It's not like that," said Manny. "You'll see."

They pulled up in front of No Place Like Home.
Click!

Manny jumped out. He ran up to the waitress standing out front and gave her a big hug.
Click!

Lenny gulped.

"We know the management." Manny's dad winked at Lenny in the mirror. The waitress walked Manny to the taxi, then got in!

"What's going on?" Lenny asked as Manny's dad kissed the waitress.

"Mama, meet Lenny," Manny said.

Lenny was speechless.

"Your mom said you can stay for dinner,"
Manny's mom said to Lenny. "I hope you
like pastel de pollo."
Click!

"Is that pastel-colored chicken?" Lenny asked Manny.

Manny howled. "Try chicken pot pie."

"It was the lunch special and didn't sell out," Mama explained.

"Does your mom always bring dinner home?" asked Lenny.

"Unless she works a double shift," Manny answered.

"Yum," said Lenny. "I wish my mom worked there."

Their taxi pulled up to a big brick building.

"Is this your *real* no place like home?" asked Lenny.

Manny nodded. "Mama and Papa picked it out when we moved here.
Click!

"Mama is really a dentist," said Manny. "But, she's not allowed to do dentist stuff here yet."

"Just like me," said Papa.

"You're a dentist, too?" asked Lenny. He ran his tongue over his teeth.

Manny laughed. "No, he's a médico, a doctor, but the rules are the same."

"I hope you don't mind sharing the homework table, Lenny," said Manny's dad. "Manny's mom and I have to study, too, so we can do our old jobs here in America."

"Cool," said Lenny. "Besides, we only have reading to a grown-up for homework."
"Bueno!" said Mama. "What are you going to read to us?"

Manny looked at Lenny. "Can I do mine at bedtime, Mama?"

"Yes," she answered.

"I'll do that, too," chimed in Lenny.

"Dinner soon," Mama said, kissing Papa.

Lenny looked at the table, full of books and papers.

"Who sets your table?"

Mama laughed. "Great timing. I was about to ask you boys to do it."

"Awww," said Manny. "Can we play first?"

"Ten minutes," said Papa.

Manny grabbed the soccer ball. He led Lenny to the park next door, doing headers all the way. **Click!**

"Wow," said Lenny. "Who taught you that?"

"My brother, Eduardo," Manny answered, passing the ball. "He plays for El Tricolor back home. He's in the National Futball League."

"Football?" asked Lenny. He missed the goal. "But who taught you soccer?"

Manny laughed. "Only Americans call it soccer."

"No way!" said Lenny, just as Papa waved them home.

When they finished dinner, a plate of sugary sticks appeared.

"What are these?" asked Lenny.

"Ever have a churro?" Manny replied.

Lenny shook his head as Manny pretended to play one like a flute.
Click!

"Yum!" said Lenny, licking cinnamon sugar off his lips. "Your mom lets you have treats?"

"Yeah, but she makes me floss after brushing," said Manny.

Mama smiled as she buzzed Lenny's mom in.

"Who reads your bedtime story?" Lenny asked as he followed Manny to the living room.

"We usually do," said Manny's dad.

"We want our English to be perfect," his mom added.

"But tonight it's my homework!" said Manny.

"One more question," said
Lenny as his mom walked in.
"Who loves you best?"

"We do!" the parents said,
with hugs all around.
Click!
"Score!" said the boys.

Student of the Week

Manny

NO PLACE LIKE Home

"I'll bring my ball so we can practice tomorrow," said Manny. Lenny grinned. "That's using your head!"